Cat Count

To all the cats I've ever known – B. L.

Betsy Lewin

Cat Count

Henry Holt and Company
New York

I have **one** cat.
A fat cat,
A fun cat.
I have one cat.

My brother has two.
Two cats,
True cats,
Wild and ballyhoo cats,
Full·of·derring·do cats.

My sister has three.
Three cats,
Glee cats,
Two of them are she cats,
The other is a he cat.

My uncle has four.
Four cats,
Store cats,
In·and·out·of·door cats.
I know someone with more cats.

My cousin has **five**.
Five cats,
Jive cats,
Very·much·alive cats.

Count them!
All together that's . . .

HOW many cats?
Fifteen.

Gram has six cats.
Fiddling·with·sticks cats,
Full·of·funny·tricks cats.

My neighbor has seven.
Seven cats,
Reveling cats,

Prowling cats and yowling cats,
Howling·to·high·heaven cats.

My teacher has **eight**.
Eight cats,
Great cats,

Proper and sedate cats,
Seldom ever late cats.

The preacher has nine.
Nine cats,
Fine cats,

Really just divine cats,
Never out-of-line cats.

The farmer has ten.
Ten cats.
TEN cats,

Chasing·duck·and·hen cats.
Count them all again—that's . . .

HOW many cats?
Fifty-five.

But wait!
There's a surprise . . .

55

My fat, fun cat
Is no longer one cat.
Add the new arrivals –

that's . . .

COUNT THE CATS

$$1 + 2 + 3 + 4 + 5 = 15$$

$$15 + 6 + 7 + 8 + 9 + 10 = 55$$

$$55 + 5 = 60$$

Henry Holt and Company, LLC, Publishers since 1866
115 West 18th Street, New York, New York 10011
www.henryholt.com

Henry Holt is a registered trademark of Henry Holt and Company, LLC
Text copyright © 1981 by Betsy Lewin
Illustrations copyright © 2003 by Betsy Lewin
Cat Count was originally published in 1981 by Dodd, Mead and Company.

Library of Congress Cataloging-in-Publication Data
Lewin, Betsy.
Cat count / by Betsy Lewin.
Summary: A child adds up the cats owned by ten different people and discovers that it is a lot of cats.
[1. Cats—Fiction. 2. Counting. 3. Stories in rhyme.] I. Title.
PZ8.3.L583 Cat 2003   [E]—dc21   2002004009

ISBN 0-8050-6747-7
First Henry Holt Edition—2003
Printed in the United States of America on acid-free paper. ∞
1 3 5 7 9 10 8 6 4 2